Kenneth Grahame's
THE WIND IN THE WILLOWS

More Adventures with Mr. Toad

Adapted by Janet Palazzo-Craig

Illustrated by Mary Alice Baer

TROLL ASSOCIATES

Library of Congress Cataloging in Publication Data

Palazzo-Craig, Janet.
    More adventures with Mr. Toad.

    (Kenneth Grahame's The wind in the willows; 3)
      Summary: The incorrigible Toad, having wrecked
seven motor-cars, is sent to prison.
    [1. Toads—Fiction]   1. Baer, Mary Alice, ill.
II. Grahame, Kenneth, 1859-1932. Wind in the willows.
III. Title.   IV Series: Palazzo-Craig, Janet. Kenneth
Grahame's The wind in the willows; 3.
PZ7.P1762Mo   [Fic]   81-16412
ISBN 0-89375-640-7 (lib. bdg.)   AACR2
ISBN 0-89375-641-5 (pbk.)

Printed in the United States of America
10 9 8 7 6 5 4 3 2

It was a bright morning in the early part of summer. The sun shone on the river as it flowed and bubbled. The Mole and the Water Rat had been up since dawn. They were busily getting ready for the first boat ride of the summer. Paddles needed mending, and their small boat needed paint.

The two friends were hard at work when the Mole heard a sound. He turned around. "Mr. Badger!" he cried. "How good to see you."

It was a wonderful thing, indeed, that the Badger should pay a call on them, or on anybody, for that matter. If you wanted him, he usually had to be caught as he slipped along the meadow early in the morning.

4

The Badger strode toward them. "The hour has come!" he said in a solemn voice.

"What hour?" asked the Rat uneasily, looking at his pocket watch.

"*Whose* hour, you should say," replied the Badger. "It's Toad's hour!"

All along the river and in the woods, the Toad was being talked about. Many months before, Toad had seen a motor-car. Instantly, he'd fallen in love with the machine. The problem was that the Toad was a terrible driver. He'd already had seven cars and seven accidents. And he'd landed in the hospital three times. But, of course, Toad thought he was an excellent driver, and no one could tell him he wasn't.

"We must go to Toad Hall and rescue our friend the Toad, before he winds up in jail," said the Badger.

"Right you are!" cried the Rat. "We'll rescue the poor, unhappy animal!"

They set off, with Badger leading the way. When they arrived at Toad Hall, a big, shiny car stood outside. It was painted red (Toad's favorite color). The Toad stood beside the car. He was dressed in goggles, a cap, and a very large overcoat.

"Hello! You're just in time for a ride," he called out cheerfully. But his smile faded when he saw the stern looks on his friends' faces.

The Badger drove the car into the garage and locked the door. Then he said, "Take him inside." The Rat and the Mole took hold of the Toad, who kicked and shouted loudly. When they succeeded in taking off his goggles and coat, he was quiet at last.

"You knew it must come to this sooner or later," the Badger explained. "Your awful driving and smash-ups and problems with the police have gone far enough. Come with me into the library. I have a few things to say to you. We'll see if you come out of that room the same Toad that you went in!"

10

The Mole and the Rat waited. In the other room, they heard the Badger's low voice talking on and on. Every once in a while, sobs could be heard.

When the door to the library opened, the Toad was drying his eyes. "Sit down, Toad," said the Badger kindly. "Friends," he announced, "I am happy to say that the Toad has seen the error of his ways."

"That is very good news, indeed," said the Rat.

"Toad," said the Badger, "promise us that you are through with cars."

There was a long silence. Toad looked this way and that. At last, he spoke. "No!" he said. "I won't. I shall never give up!"

"Very well, then," said the shocked Badger. "Take him upstairs and lock him in his bedroom."

"It's for your own good, Toady," said the Mole. And the struggling Toad was dragged up the stairs by his two faithful friends.

The Badger, Mole, and Rat took turns guarding the Toad. At first, the Toad would shout unkind things at them through the keyhole. Then he would sit on his bed making noises like a car. As time passed, though, the Toad became very quiet. His friends tried to cheer him, but nothing seemed to work. All day long, the Toad would lie in bed, staring at the walls of his room.

One fine morning, the Badger and the Mole decided to take a long walk through the woods. It was the Rat's turn to look after Toad. The Rat fixed a breakfast tray and carried it in to his friend. "How are you today?" asked the Rat.

"Thank you so much for asking," answered the Toad feebly. "But don't trouble yourself about me. I hate being a bother to my friends, and soon I won't be one."

"Is anything wrong?" asked the Rat, a little worried by Toad's weak voice.

"Oh, no," replied the Toad sadly. "Although—if I could ask one favor—but no—I don't want to trouble you—"

"What is it?" asked the Rat, truly alarmed.

"Well, I hate to bother you, but could you get a doctor for me?"

16

The Rat wondered if the Toad might be up to some sort of trick. But he did think the Toad looked a little pale. So he set off for the village, remembering first, to lock the door to Toad's bedroom.

As soon as the Toad heard the door lock, he hopped out of bed. From his window, he watched the Rat hurrying down the road. Then, laughing all the while, he put on his best suit.

He carefully tied his bedsheets to the window. Scrambling down the sheets, he set off in the opposite direction of the Rat.

"Oh, what a clever Toad!" he told himself. Very pleased with himself, the Toad strode along until he reached a little town. As he stood before an inn, he heard something. *Poop-poop!* it wailed. He saw a cloud of dust, and there it was: a beautiful motor-car. It stopped right in front of him. The riders got out and went into the inn.

As the Toad walked slowly around the car, he thought, "I wonder if this sort of car *starts* easily?" Before he knew what had happened, Toad was speeding along the road into the open countryside. Faster and faster, he went. The air rushed past him, as he joyfully sang out, "*Poop-poop! Poop-poop!*"

19

The next thing he knew, Toad was standing before a judge. "Prisoner, you have been found guilty of taking a valuable motor-car, reckless driving, and being rude to a police officer. You are sentenced to twenty years in jail!"

Bound in chains, the Toad was led away to the deepest and darkest dungeon in the land. When he heard a great door lock behind him, the Toad flung himself on the floor and sobbed. "This is the end of everything," he cried, "or, at least, it is the end of the well-liked and handsome Toad! Oh, what a stupid animal I was!" As the dreary days passed, Toad would not eat. Lying in his cell, he sobbed unhappily.

It happened that the old jailor had a young daughter, who was very fond of animals. One day, she said, "Father, I can't bear to see that poor Toad so unhappy and getting so thin. Won't you let me take care of him?" The jailor agreed. That afternoon, the girl brought a tray of hot, buttered toast into Toad's cell. "Now, cheer up, Toad," she said gently.

The Toad smelled the toast. For a moment, he thought to himself that perhaps life wasn't so bad, after all. But then he wailed and kicked and would not be comforted. The wise girl left, putting the toast near the Toad. It wasn't long before the Toad sat up and dried his eyes. After he ate the toast, he felt much better.

The young girl visited the Toad many times after that, and they became good friends. They spent many hours talking—or rather, the Toad talked and the girl listened. He told her all about Toad Hall and how much he missed it. The girl felt very sorry for Toad. She thought it was awful that he should be locked up for what seemed to her a very small mistake.

One morning, she said, "Toad, I have an aunt who is a washerwoman here at the prison." She told him her plan: dressed as the washerwoman, the Toad could walk right past the guards and escape. At first, the Toad said no—he didn't like the idea of dressing up as a washerwoman very much. But when he saw that it was his only chance, he agreed.

That night, Toad found a long dress, a shawl, and a black bonnet in his cell. Although he was scared, he put on the clothes. Slowly, he made his way through the long, dark tunnels of the dungeon. In his arms, he carried a basket of laundry. It seemed hours before he had passed through the last gate of the prison. But, at last, he was free!

He ran quickly to the train station. As he reached for his money to buy a ticket, his heart sank. He had left his coat—and all the money in it—back in the jail. Tears ran down his face as he stood alongside the train. The engineer, who was shining the engine, asked him what was wrong. "Oh, sir," cried the Toad, "I am a poor washerwoman. I've lost all my money, and I can't buy a ticket. What will I do? I must get home to my children."

The kind-hearted engineer felt sorry for the poor washerwoman. He told her she could ride with him in the engine. The Toad was very happy, as he sat beside the engineer. The train roared and rushed along. Suddenly, the engineer looked out the window of the engine. "We're being followed," he said. And, indeed, they were. Another train, full of police officers waving pistols and sticks, was close behind.

Toad fell to his knees, crying, "I must tell you the truth! Beneath these washerwoman's clothes is not a washerwoman. It is I—the well-known and popular Toad. I have just escaped from prison! I beg of you—please save me!"

The surprised engineer said, "Perhaps you *have* been a wicked Toad, but I do feel a bit sorry for you." He told the Toad of a bend in the track up ahead, where the Toad could jump to safety. When they came to the place, the engineer shouted, "Jump!"—and off the Toad flew. Hiding in some bushes, he watched both trains speed past him.

Then he laughed and laughed, rolling about on the ground and holding his sides. He was free! "Oh, what a clever Toad I am," he thought. Although he was tired and far from home, the Toad couldn't be happier. Tomorrow he would set out for Toad Hall!

Crawling beneath some bushes for shelter, he made himself a bed of leaves and twigs. And there he slept very soundly all night long.